WHO KILLED MY FAMILY?

RAJESHWARI ANDANAGIRI

TO MY

WONDERFUL DAD, MOM (WHO ARE MOST LIKELY NOT GOING TO READ THIS)

AND IRRITATING BROTHER,

I LOVE YOU

Contents

Preface *vii*

1. The Beginning Of End 1
2. The Bloodbath 6
3. The Forever Grief 9
4. The Statement 13
5. A Visit To Police Station 18
6. The Quest 26
7. In Loving Memory 30
8. Hello Serah 35
9. The Truth 41
10. One Last Time 45

Note From Author 49

Preface

Dear reader,

This book is my attempt to tell you a story without making eye contact with you.

CHAPTER ONE

THE BEGINNING OF END

Between five and six in the morning, Sara arrived home to discover our mother and father lying motionless. Undoubtedly, both of us had nightmares about that day.

I'm in my 12th standard and will be eighteen in August. I'll graduate, and then I'll be able to leave the city and start managing my own life after some time. That's what I want to do (only if my family agrees).

I'm Serah Purushottam, by the way. I'm the youngest member of the family. My older sister is the most extraordinary lady and a wonderful player (according to my family). She is Sara Purushottam, and she is five feet tall with a flawless complexion and shiny, pitch-black hair. I don't mean to seem envious, but she is stunning. She is a competitive badminton player who has won a state gold medal. (Yes, it seems quite impressive, but it was approximately three years ago, and she hasn't won even a single medal since.)

My father, Ravi Purushottam, has brown skin, a head that is half-naked, and a pleasant face. I'm not bragging, but he looks good in a suit. There are countless exciting places to work around the globe. Nevertheless, he has the most boring job. At a bank, he handles the books. Despite having what might be the dullest job, my father is a wonderful man. His company is enjoyable (not all the time though). My mother, Priya Rao, is the head of the family. Whatever choice we make must first go via her. She is a retired national-level badminton player who now works as a teacher and teaches social studies to upper-secondary students (yes, my sister gained it from her). She appears to be strict, but despite this, all of her students adore her (I'm not sure how; perhaps she has some sort of enticing charm that I must learn from).

That is my perfect family. We live on the outskirts of the city. My father prefers quiet locations with less pollution. We must, therefore, travel to the city for work, school, and other purposes. Staying miles away from the city is troublesome. I usually stay with my friends or cousins when it's too late to go home.

For four people to reside there, the house is seen to be too large. It has a duplex design, but my mother prefers a simple form, so the structure didn't look particularly attractive. It is simply white paint with a matte finish. After passing through the doorway, you will find the large greenhouse with a variety of flowers and the front door leading to the first level through stairs. We had a huge living room on the first floor, an open dining room and kitchen to the right, and our respective bedrooms on the second story. The living room was sparsely furnished and featured a large family portrait on the wall next to the room's main door on the left and a large screen television on the opposite side of the wall. The room is fairly small, even with a sofa and a rocker.

On the lawn, we grow a substantial amount of our own vegetables. My mother enjoys growing fruits and vegetables. Her plants are more important than we are (I'm not sure if that's a joke or not). She has tomatoes, green chilies, coriander, mint, lettuce, spinach, a pomegranate, guava, and mango tree.

We lead basic lifestyles. And everyone is busy working according to their daily schedule. We always eat supper together so that we can catch up on each other's days, and we hardly ever go out on the weekends. We prefer to watch movies in theatres most of the time.

Like everyday, we were having dinner at 9:45 p.m. My father was seated to my left and my mother was across from me. We had to call Sara to find out when she would be back when I realised over dinner that she was at her friend's place.

"Right, get your phone," Mother said.

I went to my room to get the phone and sat back down in my chair.

I rang her phone number. It has a quick dial. She answered the phone after two rings and said, "Hello, no funny stuff." "Hit straight to the point."

I said, "Phone's on speaker." Speak clearly. "

"Oh, tell me!" she snapped, attempting to sound composed yet agitated.

It is now late; when will you be returning home? our father asked.

"Uh! I won't be at home tonight, Dad. I'm going to hang out at my friend's place. " My sister retorted, "I'll be back at daybreak."

My father immediately replied, “alright!” without giving it a second thought. He advised her to remain cautious and take care, and cut the call.

I got into a conversation with my father after we finished talking with my sister.

“Why can’t I stay out so simply with permission?” I said furiously.

My parents have both made the same clone statement to me: “You are a child!”

“Yes, I am the only KID,” I retorted snidely. I returned immediately to my room after finishing dinner.

I knew very little, other than the fact that it was the last discussion we had with our parents.

We struggle to satisfy our daily aspirations and needs while juggling competing obligations, such as jobs. We simply follow a structured routine everyday. It must be very similar to other families, I suppose.

We went about our daily business. The frequent arguments my mother had with my father over cleaning the basement appeared natural. Sara, displaying her gold medal from three years ago. I’m attempting to ignore everything as I plan my escape from the house.

However, that evening, everything that was typical had changed. Our laughter vanished; a lifetime of suffering had replaced all the joy. My life is a complete disaster because of that evening. Our happy life ended the morning my sister discovered my parents’ bodies inside the house. Someone had slain them. They were coated in blood. Dad is in the living

room, while mom is in the kitchen.

And who? Who would act that way? Why?

CHAPTER TWO

THE BLOODBATH

My sister got home at approximately 30 minutes after seven in the morning. She began yelling for me and howling in grief as soon as she got inside the house. I was so exhausted that I had trouble making out her tone. Only garbled shouts were audible to me since I was in a trance. When I realised Sara was the one yelling out, I jumped out of bed and quickly changed into my dressing robes.

My sister and I were a little distant. The area alarmed me to my left. I could not let my attention wander or accept what I saw in the living room. My body felt stiff, and my feet were broken. I yearned to move closer to my sister, but could not do so. I was trying to speak up, but I couldn't get a word out. My heart was really pounding badly. I wanted to shout and wail, but... I stood motionless there.

I saw my father covered in blood; his face was covered in bruises. His hands had been hammered against the wall. I moved forward calmly and looked for my mum. Even if moving forward was difficult, I persisted in trying with all my strength. I could not look up as I approached the kitchen door. She appeared to be having a nap as she lay still on the chair with her head resting on the table and her back facing the kitchen door.

I forced a "Mum?" sound out of my mouth to address her.

I received nothing in exchange. My sister came and hurried to the kitchen after I tried to call my mother from the door. Sara also began calling her mother.

She continued, "Mom... mom... Mum, (she sobbed loudly and moved forward), mum," she sobbed harshly.

Sara moved closer to the table, grabbed my shoulder, and then, as she turned to face our mother, Sara fell to her knees. She intensified her sobbing. She spoke loud enough for the passing cars to hear her. I approached her and pulled her up by the legs.

My mother was lying there dead when I saw her. She suffered a neck cut. Her forehead had been harmed. She appeared to be telling the offender that she was willing to die with a smile on her face.

I dropped to my knees. Even though my heart was broken, I remained dry-eyed. I wanted to sob. I had the sensation that someone had struck and broken my heart. I could feel my insides tightening and my heart pounding, but I couldn't put words to the experience or utter it aloud. My thoughts were scattered, and I was unable to understand what had occurred or what was happening to me.

I ended up staying there for at least 45 minutes before standing up. I called the police and told them what we had seen over the phone.

I started rearranging my thoughts before the cops arrived, considering every imaginable scenario and potential perpetrator of this heinous deed. I could not conceive even one name.

After a short while, it became clear that it could have been a burglar who attempted to loot but was apprehended.

He may resort to bloodshed in order to defend himself.

I jumped to my feet and began searching for any lost valuables at home. To my surprise, everything was in its original location.

I tried writing every possible story to solve what happened, but I was unsuccessful.

Based on what I've seen and observed, I believe my parents are good people. They have always helped others and have never been ill-tempered to anyone. I'm not sure what happened to our family. Who and why would they wreak such havoc on our lives?

CHAPTER THREE

THE FOREVER GRIEF

After the police call ended, I called our uncle and aunt to come over right away. They were the only ones that caught my eye. My parents did not get along with any of my maternal or paternal relatives, including our grandparents. As a result, we didn't have many relatives. And we didn't have much contact with them. In fact, I've never seen most of them.

The uncle I contacted is my father's childhood friend, and they are absolutely dear, completely like family.

Our uncle is a retired professor. He has 15 plus years of experience in the teaching field. Now, he gives cost-less career guidance to students online. His first name is David, and we never heard either dad or mom call him that. They picked the nickname "Grey" over his first name.

And his companion, our aunt, is a homemaker. She dedicated all her soul to taking care of the household. My parents weren't on good terms with their families because they moved against their agreement and had an inter-caste marriage. Just like my parents, my uncle and aunt were not on good terms with their families, but they still maintained a normal connection and visited them occasionally. Their marriage was inter-religion. Shriya, my aunt, being a Hindu, and David, my uncle, being a Christian, progressed from schoolmates to college mates to couples to life partners.

Five minutes past nine, the police appeared at our residence. My aunt and uncle arrived precisely on time, a moment after the arrival of the police. They were surprised to see what had happened to mom and dad. As soon as my aunt came in, she seized me and Sara in her arms. We were in the living room, and my uncle was talking with a tall man who sounded like he was in charge and the chief.

There were around three police officers. A tall, muscular gentleman who seemed fit, healthy and mostly had grey hair. He was the head of everyone who reported him on the scene. The assistant looked like he should have been in the hospital rather than working. He appeared pale and anemic. He kept accompanying the tall gentleman wherever he went and taking instructions from him. A middle-aged woman, who had a comforting feeling, was implied to be the lowest ranking police officer among the people who turned up.

The forensic team arrived after the police examined the area around the house and at the spot. As soon as they appeared, they began collecting blood samples, fingerprints, and whatever else was crucial for the investigation.

In mid-afternoon, the sun was shining on top of my head. The pale assistant who was standing in the garden was talking to the head and looked as if the tall guy was giving instructions. The head appeared serious, and the assistant was sweating heavily, not sure if he was because of the sun or what. As soon as they finished talking, the assistant rushed towards my sister.

The forensics team was in the backyard with the aunt and uncle to help them identify the ins and outs of the house.

Once the assistant entered the living room, he started speaking with a high-pitched voice, as if he were investigating a criminal. Rather than a formal inquiry, he reacted irritably and loudly.

When my sister heard such a pitch, her tears burst into a fit of rage that exceeded the sound of the pale assistant's high-pitched voice. A quick response from our uncle pulled the assistant from my sister, just as he rushed out the front door. It's easy to judge my uncle by how strong he is. He's as strong as a professional bodyguard. The assistant fell to the ground after falling on his back toward the wall.

"AAAHHH! "That hurts," said the assistant as he struggled to stand on his own two feet.

Taking a hand to help the assistant stand, Uncle said, "I'm sorry officer, we know you would like to know the situation better, but there needs to be a proper way."

"Ah!" replied the tall officer. I apologise for the inconvenience. Sorry. I might sound rude..."

Our aunt raced over and shoved past the female cop who was waiting at the entrance to the living room before the officer could complete his sentence, and she suddenly wrapped us in her arms, listening to her yell, "Don't you dare shout at my kids!"

I've never seen our aunt so enraged; I expected her to be calm and attentive to the officer, but she understood us. She knew we needed time to gather our thoughts before answering the officer's questions; she knew we were heartbroken and couldn't speak.

My sister had stopped crying and was wiping her tears away. For a moment, she and I locked gazes.

"Children, are you guys all right?" our aunt inquired quietly, as if whispering.

I hadn't cried since the morning, when I felt a heavy hit in my chest and my throat felt like it was being strangled; as I looked at my aunt, tears streamed down my face. I couldn't help but cry. I cried for an hour and a half, murmuring something that neither my aunt nor anyone else could understand. But she continued to pat my back and hug me, giving me slow pats on the head. I stopped crying when I had hiccups.

I didn't notice much because I had been crying, but my sister stopped crying and was constantly patting me. My aunt asked if we wanted to rest or continue with the investigation.

I didn't want to answer the police questions, but I also wanted to get out of the situation as soon as possible.

Both my sister and I said "Yes" simultaneously.

Aunt stood up and whispered something to the tall police officer as she motioned him out into the garden. I attempted to eavesdrop but was unsuccessful.

While I was crying, the cops went through the house looking for signs of intruders and hints of evidence. And they wrapped the bodies in order to proceed with the autopsy.

My sister and I were sitting on the sofa in the living room, and the female officer sat next to us. After a few moments of silence, she spoke quietly and sweetly, asking, "Do you want to eat something?"

CHAPTER FOUR

THE STATEMENT

"No, I'm not hungry," I whispered, looking at her face.

"Yes, we'll eat," my sister replied. "Could you please get something from the kitchen for us?"

The lady replied sweetly, "Of course," and started walking towards the kitchen, leaving me and Sara alone. Before the lady returned, my aunt came back to check on us. She sat beside Sara and whispered something to her.

In a few minutes, the lady returned with biscuits, milk, and some fruit. I wasn't particularly hungry, but Sara and my aunt persuaded me to eat. We wrapped the leftover snacks and put them away about 20 minutes later.

The assistant arrived 18 minutes past one to ask us the questions.

He didn't appear or sound rude this time. He sounded like a concerned adult, but the fear on his face was obvious. He took a notepad and a pen from his handbag and prepared himself to write down whatever we discussed.

"Are you feeling okay now?" he asked my sister.

"Yes," Sara said.

"May I begin with your name and your relationship to the victims?" The assistant stated

"I am Sara Purushottam. She is my sister, Serah Purushottam," my sister said, slightly nodding her head. "Ravi Purushottam and Priya Rao are our parents."

The assistant inquired about our parents' occupations and who was the first to notice the incident.

She briefly described our parents' jobs, stating that our mother is a teacher and our father works in a bank. Tears fell from her eyes as she began to speak about the incident. "It was early morning when I returned home (paused for a moment and continued) from my friend's place after a night out," she said slowly, breaking down and sobbing after each word.

"And...

And I '

And I used my keys to enter the house; as soon as I entered..., I called for my father but received no response; so, I went in, into the main hall, and saw..."

My sister fell silent for a few minutes and continued mumbling while sobbing, which none of us understood, but we knew she was in pain because the assistant and the lady police officer didn't interrupt and let her cry. She continued, "I saw dad's hands hammered to the wall," pointing to the wall, "and I... I... started crying and calling my sister, and she rushed down as soon as she heard me."

"And then what happened?" The assistant inquired as to my sister, and fell silent once more.

I explained, "I rushed down as soon as I heard her wailing, and I was shocked by what I had seen and felt ice-cold." I looked for my mother and later found her in the kitchen, with her head resting on the dining table and sitting in the chair. "

While we were explaining, the assistant scribbled everything in his notepad as quickly as he could.

The Aunt stood beside the assistant while he took notes, and now and then she looked at us and said, "It's okay, it'll be alright."

He looked at me as he finished his last note and asked, "Did your parents fight the night before?"

"No," I replied, puzzled as to why he had asked the question.

"Do they have any disagreements or problems between them?" he inquired once more.

"No, not at all. They were great, and they loved each other, "I snarled."

"How are your parents?" "Do you believe someone is planning to harm them?" He went on.

I was at a loss for words. All I know is that our parents are the nicest people you'll ever meet, and they're always friendly and ready to help someone in need. I looked the assistant in the eyes for a moment before saying, "no."

The assistant looked at me as if he wanted more information, but I didn't respond. Then he turned to our aunt, who was sitting beside us, and gave the assistant a warning look so he wouldn't be rude to us again. The aunt's warning look appeared to have scared the assistant.

"This will suffice," he said, and continued in hushed tones, "I'm sorry about earlier."

"It's my higher ups who wanted to rush the case and wanted me to be rude enough to get information fast." "I was tough on you," said the assistant.

He stood up and approached the police chief, who was standing in the garden.

He stood up right away. I noticed our uncle conversing with the police chief, and they appeared to be deep in conversation.

As the assistant went to the police chief, Uncle shook their hands and returned to where we were sitting, asking if we were okay and continuing to tell us that we needed to proceed with the funeral preparations. He stated that the police will take the bodies for autopsies and return them to us by tomorrow so that we can plan the funeral.

We said nothing. We simply remained silent and nodded in response to every question and statement they made.

The ambulance arrived for the autopsy of my deceased mother and father.

While returning to the front gate, the head pointed to a plant in the garden and asked the assistant to dig because it was the only freshly planted plant and the police suspected the culprit had hidden something more like a murder weapon beneath the plant.

I interrupted them as the helper came over to dig up the plant. "Mom planted it yesterday, and it has nothing to do with the culprit," I explained.

"Let's just ensure there is nothing wrong and we are not missing anything," the head stated.

"No, that's the last one mom planted, and I don't want you guys to destroy it," I retorted angrily.

"Sir, just let it be," the uncle added.

"All right," the cop said. They started walking towards the main gate.

I overheard the police talking as they were returning. One of them stated that there was no sign of any intruders. And the perpetrator could be someone who knows their way around the house.

Those words have been running through my head since I overheard the cops talk. I began to consider everyone we knew in and around our house. There were people who knew the area around our house, but not everyone can get in so easily and leave no trace of their intrusion.

CHAPTER FIVE

A VISIT TO POLICE STATION

The next two days were hell. Most of the time, I didn't leave my room. I pretended nothing had happened and remained motionless in the room. My aunt brought the food into my room as I barely came out. Sara continued to accompany our aunt on her chores. Sara tried to cheer me up and get me out of the room, but I refused. The world outside my room appeared dull and depressing. I needed my space to deal with reality.

The funeral arrangements were made, I noticed a lot of people coming from Mom and Dad's workplace. I didn't recognize at least 10% of the attendees. There was no sign of our relatives; perhaps this piece of information never reached them, or if it did, they ignored it. Our aunt and uncle took everything care of. And preferred that we stay with our parents. And we performed the cremation rites at 11:50 AM. Being the oldest daughter, Sara delivered the last rites.

I saw a few police officers during the funeral procession, and they remained until the rites were completed.

We will receive the autopsy report in a week. One of the female cops who attended the service informed us.

After the rituals were completed, our parents were laid to rest in a graveyard seven kilometres from our house.

After everything was over, my aunt and uncle and I went back home. My aunt got to work organising and cleaning as we settled into the living room. The environment in the room had the consistency of thick, cold custard.

Uncle said, "You guys should come home with us," breaking the awkward silence, "Stay with us as we work things out for a few days."

Our aunt joined him and added, "Yes, it will change your environment and you can experience a different atmosphere."

"All right," Sara said, her voice drab and worn out.

We weren't even sure if it was safe to stay because there was nothing for us to do here and the situation was unclear. We decided to go with my aunt and uncle.

Only the sound of moving cars could be heard in the room once more.

My aunt and uncle remained in the living room while Sara and I went upstairs to pack our belongings.

After about 15 to 20 minutes, we returned downstairs with our packed luggage. The aunt and uncle were speaking as they sat down, but they came to a halt when they noticed us.

"So, have you got everything you need packed, children?" Uncle asked.

"Uh, yes," I countered.

Okay, let's lock the door and leave, suggested the aunt. Come over, and I'll help you load your bags into the car, "replied Aunt."

Sara, my aunt, and I each left the room with one bag, which we put in the car. The uncle later locked the main room and gate before leaving the house.

Aunt sat in the passenger seat as Uncle began the engine. We were both in the rear row. Neither my aunt nor uncle said anything to us the entire journey.

We had to travel for over three hours to get to my uncle and aunt's house in the city. I slept the entire trip because I was so tired.

As soon as we got to my aunt's house, she woke me up. When I finally opened my eyes, Sara and Uncle had already left, so I went upstairs with Aunt.

My aunt's house had three bedrooms, a kitchen, a dining area, and a small reading room. The living area was really vibrant, thanks to the artwork and flower vase on the table. The indoor plants added a light, breezy sense to the space.

As soon as we arrived, Uncle took us around the bedrooms, and Aunt prepared dinner. Although we had visited this location several times before, this time felt different. This time, I felt disconnected. It was difficult to feel at peace.

Based on her actions, Sara appeared to be feeling the same way I was. "You should sleep now; we'll speak about everything tomorrow," Uncle said after we finished eating.

"But..." I tried to say.

Nothing to say right now. Rest. My uncle cut me off.

Auntie got up from her chair, kissed both of our foreheads, and whispered good night to us.

We went to our bedrooms after saying "good night, aunt and uncle."

The first night here was challenging. I was having difficulty sleeping. I went off to bed and knocked on my sister's bedroom door.

She inquired, "What happened?" Are you alright? Is there something upsetting you?" A little while after opening the door, in an unsettling manner.

It was exhausting to listen to her ask so many questions without even pausing.

With a sigh, I responded, "I'm OK, let me in."

I walked in after she stepped aside.

"I couldn't sleep, so I came over to check on you," I explained as I sat back down on her bed.

"Oh, okay," she said, pausing slightly before adding, "I think I'm okay."

After that, we said little. That night, I slept next to her.

We waited a few days and received no information from the police. The lady officer contacted us one morning, saying that the autopsy report had arrived, and we needed to visit the police station before the evening.

After lunch, Uncle urged us to get ready so that we could go to the police station.

We arrived at the station 12 minutes past one. They requested we meet with the station's manager, and we had to wait for almost half an hour because he was busy.

There were only two chairs available. Uncle and aunt sat in front of the writer's desk. Sara and I stood impatiently behind them.

The time is two o'clock. We've been waiting for over thirty minutes. I couldn't take it any longer and went to ask one of the lady constables on the right-side table of the writer.

"Excuse me, ma'am, when can we meet with the chief officer?" I said.

"Wait a minute, let me ask sir if he's ready," she said.

She got out of her chair and walked over to the door that said, "Sanjeev Shetty, chief officer."

She gently knocked three times on the door.

After a few minutes, she came out and asked to go in.

Sara and I followed my aunt and uncle to the chief officer's room. Uncle knocked twice and received a response of "yes, please come in."

My uncle said, "Hello" respectfully as we all entered.

With a smile on his face, the head replied, "hello," and added, "please, you can sit," pointing his hands towards the chair. My uncle and aunt were seated in front of the chief officer. And we were once again standing behind them.

"I'm sorry for your loss," the head said, his smile fading. "If I'm not mistaken, you're both the daughters of a deceased couple," he added.

"Yes," Sara said.

Observing uncle and aunt, "Are you now the legal guardian of both?" The Chief inquired.

The Uncle said simply, "Yes."

"OK, that's excellent to hear," remarked the head, looking at the few papers in front of him and continuing, "so, how are you related to them?"

"My husband and their parents are family friends." "He has been friends with Ravi since they were children," the aunt responded this time.

"Okay, so, as you heard, the autopsy report is done," remarked Head, nodding his head. I'm working on this matter, and I'll get back to you with the specifics. "

"Sure," the uncle said.

"I want the kids to stay outside and wait while we talk," the chief added.

"No, they are our parents." "We have every right to know what happened to them," I retorted immediately.

To my surprise, Uncle agreed with my decision, saying, "Sir, they are not children, and they deserve to know what actually happened, so let them stay."

"All right, anything you want to do," said the Chief.

He began going over the stack of documents on the table in front of him. After a minute, he pressed a small umbrella-shaped bell beside him, and a peon entered the room.

The person who came in was dressed in khaki pants and a shirt, and he appeared pale and frail, as if he hadn't been eating properly.

"Rao uncle, can you bring two additional seats and water for the girls?" the chief said as he entered.

"OK, no problem," the person said. He exited the room and returned two minutes later with chairs. He stepped out again, placing one beside my aunt and one beside my uncle.

"Please sit," the chief said.

I sat to Uncle's right, while Sara sat to Aunt's left. We were sitting when the door was knocked again, and this time the peon came in with four cups of water. He placed one in front of each of us.

I muttered, "Thank you."

"Not a problem, kid," the peon said as he looked me in the eye. He then exited the room.

The chief straightened his shoulders as he prepared to speak.

He said, "I realise it's awful to lose the family. It's difficult to hear, but we have to get through this, so, yeah! Let's start with the crime site, where there was no evidence of a violent intrusion. Someone who has been visiting the family regularly or someone they know could be the culprit. Other than the family members' fingerprints, forensics discovered no other prints. And the weapon used by the perpetrator is still missing. "

I tried hard not to cry while the head was speaking, but I couldn't stop myself; tears streamed down my cheeks. I glanced left to find my sister, Sara, and aunt also crying.

The Chief paused for a moment before motioning to the water and saying, "Please, control yourselves and have some water."

"I know it's difficult, but you have to stay strong for the sake of the kids," he added, looking at my aunt.

Our Aunt began wiping her tears away and took a glass of water from the table with her right hand, wiping Sara's tears with the left.

Before my aunt or uncle could console me, I stopped crying.

My uncle gently rubbed my back twice and, holding my left hand, asked the Chief, "Sir, when do you believe you'll be able to uncover the real culprit?"

"Yes, sir," the chief said. We'll do everything we can to discover the perpetrator of this act, but first, could you provide us with some information? "

"Sure, sir, anything I can do," Uncle answered.

"Do you suspect anyone—I mean, if they ever had any enemies, or someone who didn't want them to live?" inquired the Chief.

"Oh! No, sir, they had no enemies. They were always kind and kind-hearted, and we don't think anyone we know would do this, "Uncle answered, glancing at aunt.

"Certainly," the aunt added.

"Okay, thank you for coming all the way here; we'll attempt to figure out who's behind this as soon as possible," the Chief stated.

"Sir, please find the culprit as soon as possible, and thank you," Uncle said.

Once again, the chief pressed the bell, and a peon hurried in. He requested the peon to call the station subhead, and the subhead arrived as quickly as the peon had.

The Chief requested Anurag, entitled Sub-head, to accompany us out.

While we were leaving, the Chief said, "Excuse me sir, if you require any help in the future, please call Mr. Anurag. He's the sub-head here."

"Alright, sure, thank you," Uncle said.

We left the station, and Uncle got the subhead's contact information before departing for our aunt's house.

CHAPTER SIX

THE QUEST

It's been over a month since our parents died, but the police have provided no information about the perpetrator. The bank fraud was exposed on the same day my parents were murdered, and every form of media focused on it. The police were more concerned with that case and ignored ours.

We lived at my uncle and aunt's house for a few weeks before moving back to our house with Aunt and Uncle. We looked for any hints or signs that could lead us to the offender. We looked through our parents' belongings, emails, phones, and anything else that would hint at who it could be.

My sister took my mother's, whereas I took my father's. While I was looking through my father's laptop in our parents' now-dusty room, Sara took our mother's few files, laptop, and phone and left the room to go back to the living room. I soon noticed a folder labelled "Love." When I opened it, it was password restricted. I entered my sister's birth date to see if it would open, but it didn't. My mother's birthday was supposed to come next, but it didn't. I placed mine in the last chance slot, and it opened.

The number of videos astounded me. Each video is labelled with the month and year in order. It contained approximately 180 videos.

Why does he have so many videos? What did our parents want to keep hidden from us?

My mind was racing with questions, so I opened the videos before addressing my sister.

When I opened the most recent one, I couldn't believe what I saw with my own eyes. My thoughts were scattered, and I couldn't think straight.

I pulled out a chair and sat down. I shutdown the laptop while still thinking about the videos. I was so lost in my own thoughts that when my sister gave me a tiny push from behind, I was terrified to death.

She was right behind me and not too far away. She came in and I had not even seen her.

"I found nothing relevant on the mom's laptop," she remarked, putting her right hand on my shoulder from behind.

I was hesitant to tell her what I had observed. I decided not to tell her until I figured out what was going on. As a result, I did not respond to her. And I fell silent.

"Are you okay?" she asked, softly patting my shoulder.

I replied, "Yes."

"Are you sure?" She inquired once more.

"Yes," I replied hesitantly.

"Did you come across anything unusual?" my sister asked again, comfortingly, as if she knew something was wrong.

I felt like I was betraying her by not telling her what I witnessed, but I didn't want her to know for her own safety.

"No, I said." in a tired, sluggish voice.

Sara responded, "It is fine, Let's just eat and sleep and try again tomorrow."

We returned everything to its proper position and went downstairs for dinner. Sara went to see our aunt, who was cooking in the kitchen. I went into the living room and sat silently, puzzled why my father kept them.

The more I thought about it, the more I was sure I had not heard my aunt's repeated requests for food. I was startled and gasped in amazement when my aunt enquired, "What happened?" with a worried scowl on her face.

"Um, nothing." I lied. To be honest, the unexpected pat scared me to death because I wasn't paying attention to what was going on in the kitchen or living room and was lost in my own thoughts.

"Are you okay?" My aunt asked me once more, gently stroking my hair.

"Oh! "Yes," I lied again and continued, "So, dinner's ready?"

"Come on, come on!" Aunt responded.

We ate our dinner in complete silence. We finished in about a half-hour and went back to our rooms.

My aunt and uncle were using the guest room as usual, so we returned to our own room.

The night felt darker, and it was another strange, uncomfortable night to sleep in. I had trouble falling asleep. Every new plausible explanation has brought back memories of everything I've seen. It lost me in all those incomprehensible ideas, and I did not know when I fell asleep.

I awoke exhausted the next morning around 13 minutes past 8 a.m. When I awoke, I went straight to the kitchen to ask my aunt if she needed help to make breakfast.

"Good morning, sweetie," my aunt greeted me as I entered the kitchen. "Did you have a good sleep?"

I have definitely lied, "Good morning, yes."

"Can I help with anything here?" I asked, not wanting my aunt to worry any more.

"That's wonderful to hear, sweetie," she said, motioning to the freshly made bread and the knife next to it. "Cut me some pieces."

"Sure," I replied.

"In the meantime, I'll get Sara up; she wanted me to get her up, but I let her sleep in." replied Aunt.

"I hear she's been having difficulties sleeping," my aunt added.

I said half-heartedly, "Oh, yes! Yes, "

"Be careful with the knife," the aunt advised as she exited the kitchen.

As she walked away, I took the bread and began cutting it. And I looked at Uncle through the kitchen window. He was reading the newspaper while sitting in the garden. After a few seconds, I resumed cutting the bread.

Before I could finish, I heard my aunt shouting from upstairs. My uncle and I ran upstairs together.

It's Sara now.

Her bed sheets were covered in blood and her wrist was cut.

CHAPTER SEVEN

IN LOVING MEMORY

I left the knife and bread unfinished to go upstairs as soon as I heard Aunt shouting, and Uncle came dashing inside, tossing the newspaper aside in the garden.

My uncle took the lead, and I followed close behind. When I arrived upstairs, my aunt was on her knees at my sister's door; my uncle didn't enter the room, didn't answer, and said nothing. He assisted my aunt in standing on her own legs.

I was having strange thoughts. I took a small step forward to look, but my aunt stood in front of me, horrified, and said, "no."

I couldn't stop myself, so instead of having all these crazy notions, I looked at what actually happened. So, I told Aunt, "It's okay, Aunt, I'll be fine."

Uncle hinted for Aunt to step back. And she did.

I never expected her to do this to me. She has always surprised me by being both academically and physically strong. I had the impression that I was never there for her in her moments of need, when she was suffering, or when she was frightened. The feeling of guilt for letting anything like this happen filled me up.

Only if I had gone to her room the night before, would she still be here, having breakfast with us.

With all those thoughts racing through my mind, hating myself for not being there for Sara, I was furious. I entered the room with tears streaming down my cheeks. My aunt tried to stop me, but I continued going.

She was lying on her bed with her legs out of bed, dressed in her nightgown, holding a knife in her right hand and a paper note in her left. I repositioned her legs on the bed and draped a blood-splattered bed sheet over her body.

I removed the paper from her clinched left palm and read it. In a rage, I snatched the knife from her grip and threw it away.

I got down on my knees, pressed the paper against my chest, and couldn't stop crying. Uncle and Aunt entered the room, and while Uncle took the paper from my hands, Aunt tried to calm me down by hugging me and carefully caressing my back.

I never imagined losing all of my family members in such a short period. I was not just sad; I felt as if I were dead, as if I would never be able to feel happy again.

I sat in a corner in her room. Meanwhile, Uncle dialed the police. The police arrived at half past ten.

Since our parents died a month and a half ago, the authorities assumed Sara committed suicide because of depression. In addition, there is a paper note referred to as a "suicide letter." They sent the knife to forensics for fingerprints. And nothing else made them suspicious, so they closed the investigation, labelling it suicide.

We held the funeral the next day, and I performed all the last rites. We returned to the city after completing all the formalities, to my uncle and aunt's house.

I didn't want to go out once we got back, so I shut myself in my room and just came out for meals.

I said little at all during the meals. To be more specific, I did not know how or what I was experiencing. The silence surrounding me has given me a strange comfort.

My uncle suggested I see a therapist because the last six months have been an immense shock to me and it would help me mentally get stronger.

The first attempt to get me to go to counselling failed completely. I didn't even respond and walked out of the room in the middle of the conversation.

During an afternoon lunch, Uncle said, "I know it's difficult to accept, but you need to keep going. There's a lot waiting for you in the future, and you shouldn't quit easily." He didn't look at me while speaking. He continued, "The pain you're going through is enormous, and you need to let it out someday or other before it turns toxic."

"I also understand that I have no right to interfere in your life," he explained, "but I am doing it because I always want the best for you and consider you as my child."

I've always thought of my uncle as a figure second to my father, and because we didn't have many relatives, I've spent much of my leisure time with them. After hearing from Uncle that afternoon, I realised he'd been more than a parent to me.

"All right, we'll get started today," I immediately said, with tears in my eyes.

"Please don't cry, my darling; you are our daughter." My aunt said this while tenderly caressing my hair and wiping my tears.

I just nodded. Although I have lost my family, I still have my extended family to look forward to. I'll locate the culprit as soon as I've determined to live for my family, aunt, and uncle's dreams.

My first session with the therapist was that evening. She's an auntie's acquaintance who also knew my parents. The session lasted an hour and a half. My uncle dropped me off and then picked me up. He even purchased an ice cream tub to cheer me up after the session.

We said nothing on the drive back home.

"Are you alright?" Uncle asked.

"Yes," I said.

"Here's some ice cream for you," Uncle said, pointing to the tub of ice cream in the back-seat.

"Thank you very much." With a smile, I responded.

We had dinner and watched a television show once we got home. After a while, I said both aunt and uncle good night and went to my room.

"Serah, come here," my aunt said as I was walking to my room.

I turned around and returned to her.

"Good night, dear; if it is too much for you, come to me; we will talk," she said as she kissed my brow.

"Sleep well," I said, nodding.

"Alright, good night," she said.

I returned to my room, knowing that there was still someone out there who cared about me. They will protect and cherish me, and I will not be alone.

We returned to my aunt's place after Sara's death. I brought dad's laptop with me. As it was the only item that had something suspicious to deal with, the videos could lead to the culprit.

I opened my father's laptop and opened the "Love" folder, where I typed my birthday as the password and began watching videos one after the other. After an hour or two, I understood it was pointless to watch every video;

instead, I should prioritise the most current ones and view the rest later if necessary. So, I looked up the date of my parents' deaths. The video, which was dated in the month of my parents' death, shocked me. I was sweating profusely, terrified, and my heart was pounding so loudly that I could hear it.

I shut down the laptop and began to ponder a swarm of questions, and I couldn't even figure out one answer. I started writing down every thought, action, and possible conclusion I saw in the video.

"WHO ARE YOU?" was the last thing I scribbled in the notebook before falling asleep there on the chair and reading table.

CHAPTER EIGHT

HELLO SERAH

I finally woke up at about eight o'clock in the morning to the sound of birds chirping outside my window. Having birds around isn't always nice. Pigeon hooters are noisy and will never let you sleep peacefully.

I distinctly remember falling asleep on a chair near the reading table, but I awoke in my bed. I had no recollection of having to get up and sleep in bed.

I got out of bed, straining my head to figure out how I ended up on the bed. I approached the table gently and was surprised to discover a response to my previous night's question, "WHO ARE YOU?"

"Check the videos on your phone," the reply said.

I was terrified to learn that there had been a second person in the room the night before. I was wondering who it was, but I didn't check right away.

I wanted to tell my aunt that I was fine, but that I needed a little more sleep so she would not bother me later.

I exited my room to find my uncle reading the newspaper with soft music playing in the background, as is his custom, and my aunt in the kitchen preparing breakfast. When I walked in, she had her radio on and was humming to some 90's pop music.

My heart was racing fast, but I tried to appear normal. As I approached the kitchen, I knocked slowly and hesitantly on the door, and Aunt turned back, saying, "Oh, dear, you are up."

"Are you alright?" Is there something bothering you? "Are you feeling sick?" My aunt started asking questions, one after the other.

"No, no, no, no... I'm okay. "It's just that I wanted to rest a bit more and I didn't want breakfast. I'll be up by lunch time," I replied.

"Oh, it is fine, but no skipping breakfast; eat and go to bed," Aunt said, adding, "but remember, if you need anything else or want to talk about something, remember I am here."

"Sure," I replied.

I ate the sandwiches and milk as quickly as I could in the next 15 minutes so that I could return to my room. As I completed my meal, I stood up and hurriedly headed to my room, saying, "Thank you for the food." I'll rest up now. "Bye aunt, and have a good day at work, uncle. "

My uncle said, "Thank you, sweetie, and have a wonderful day as well."

"Come to me if you need anything," my aunt said loudly as I walked by.

I entered my room, locked the door, sat on my bed, and opened my phone. I searched for the most recent video and discovered it.

I played it immediately; I was the one who was speaking on the video. My eyes couldn't believe what they were seeing. It's someone that looks precisely like me, right down to the hair and clothing. Why couldn't I recall anything if it was me? Is it possible that I have a twin?

My thoughts raced through my mind.

"Uh! "Hi" in an excited voice, "I never imagined you were truly this dumb to know who I am." in a mocking tone, "okay, forget it." I'm Ray, and sure, I look like you; in fact, I live inside you."

In disbelief, I paused the video. What? Live inside me? I puzzled, "Why do I have a different personality, and why don't I remember anything?" Every question that kept popping into my head was annoying.

"Sounds strange, doesn't it?" Ray said as I continued the video. Nah! Not at all; it's more like a sort of entertainment for me. "

What? Entertainment? I wondered aloud. She irritated me, and my insides flamed with anger for Ray.

"But it's extremely bothersome to live like this. I want to live freely, like, going out, making friends, having a family and everything, but you know, your parents, oh!" The video said, "I mean, our parents, they wouldn't let me out." What!!!! Did my mom and dad know about you? Why didn't they tell me about this? Is this why Father set up the camera in our house? So, every video on the father's laptop is about only her, Ray.

I felt like punching a hole in the wall; I was so furious. My anger and frustration have now reached a whole new level.

I kept watching the video in between all of my strange thoughts and explanations for the questions I'd been jotting down. They would not let me out. I agree that they are wonderful parents. They gave me affection, but only for a limited period. They let me out, but only for a limited period, and it is difficult to do everything in the time they've given me. So, I approached them and said, "I want to live more like you, livelier and happier, studying, going out, and having fun like everyone else."

Of course, my parents would never agree to this; they'd never allow me to sacrifice my life for someone who appears and then vanishes, I thought to myself.

"But they said no," the video continued (see, I knew they'd say no, I told myself), "So I pleaded, tried to persuade them, but they wouldn't accept it no matter what, so I did it."

WHAT DID YOU DO? I was furious.

"I killed them. Should I offer you a little more news? " She continued. Her expression was creepy and evil.

With a sly expression on her face, she paused and giggled evilly, "I killed your sister, no, no, OUR sister," Ray stressed the word OUR.

"She's intelligent, unlike you." "You discovered the footage on Dad's laptop but refused to review it, but Sara did not," Ray said proudly.

"So, I had to kill her before she did something dumb. I've always liked her, but I had no choice. "You know, I have to protect us," she continued. "So, I made her die," she added creepily, "because she loves you, she died for you, and you better live up to her."

I burst into tears, cried to myself, and questioned myself in the mirror, "Why do you do that?" Who are you to protect me? I don't need anyone's protection. I can protect myself. I couldn't stop myself from yelling angrily, "Protect us!" Not while I'm still alive; I'll make sure you're gone for good.

I guess I've told you enough. Now I have my freedom. I've got a lot to do. "Bye," Ray remarked joyfully, and the video stopped.

I lay on my back on the bed, lost in thought. The clock had hit twelve o'clock by the time I realised I had Dad's laptop and could watch all of Ray's video footage.

Aunt knocked on my door again 30 minutes after twelve and said, "Serah, wake up. Let's eat lunch."

I didn't want to eat, but it was necessary to keep Aunt away, so I got up and opened the door.

When she saw my face, she immediately hugged me and asked, "Did you cry, dear?"

"No," I said.

"Wash up, let's eat," said the aunt.

"Alright," I replied. My thoughts are still in my room, and I cannot wait to see everything about Ray in detail. I went to the dining table as soon as I finished washing my hands. After that, I sat down to eat.

To break the unpleasant silence, I asked, "Eh! Where has Uncle gone? "

"He's at work and will probably return about five o'clock in the evening." My aunt was quick to respond.

"Okay." The silence returned to the room.

This time, Aunt broke the pause by saying, "What do you think about going to the movies or the mall in the evening once David returns?"

"No," I groaned, continuing, "I want to relax a little longer, perhaps tomorrow or the day after."

"Alright," she said, smiling.

The rest of lunch went rather smoothly. I ate as soon as I could in order to complete the search for the video footage.

I thanked my aunt and went to my room as soon as I finished my dinner.

I closed the door once again and opened Father's laptop. I looked for and opened the same "Love" file.

To my amazement, the folder now had only one video. The remaining 180 (roughly) videos have vanished.

I played the single video in the file and it appeared to be her, Ray.

She said bossily, "Hello! Once again, I knew you'd come here."

CHAPTER NINE

THE TRUTH

"I knew you'd be here wondering who I am and how I am when I'm with our parents. Is it really me who killed them, blah blah blah." She mocked.

"I wanted to help you, Serah" (a brief pause followed by a continuation). You know, there were over 100 videos, and it takes up all of your time, and you will be exhausted again and won't be able to spend time with your beloved aunt and uncle. So, I'm doing you this kindness." she said, winking with her right eye.

"You may thank me later," she smirked.

"Now, let's get to the point. What a stupid person you are. I mean, after knowing the truth, I killed our sister. How do you think I'd leave the recordings untouched?" She burst out laughing and sounded like an evil witch.

"I'm sorry for calling you dumb, but that's the truth, my girl! So, you want to know if I killed them, right? Of course, I'll tell you all the specifics. Don't worry, it was actually fun to do it," she said, her face self-aware, proud, and crafty.

"I didn't want to kill them," she said, putting on a poker expression, "but they wouldn't agree to my desires. ALL THEY THINK IS THAT YOU ARE IMPORTANT, AND ONLY YOU ARE. I asked, pleaded, and did everything I could to persuade them to give me a few days of freedom. They are as stubborn as I am and have left me with no alternative."

Ray's tone was as if she didn't care about anything anymore and would do anything to get what she wanted.

"It was dad first, oh! No, it's not mom, no, no, no, Tch! Tch! Tch! I can't recall exactly. It doesn't seem to matter right now. Anyway, our parents love you and would never allow me to harm you; they would even die for you. As a result, it is both my greatest strength and their greatest vulnerability. I played well; I promised them I'd kill myself if they didn't do as I said; if I did not live, you're not supposed to be here either. When I warned them that I was going to kill myself, I saw genuine dread and desperation in their eyes. Not because they loved me, but because their precious daughter SERAH's death terrified them. I wanted to give them a second chance, so I presented my ideas: "I'll take your body for at least two days a week, which means you will voluntarily give me your body and disappear silently with all your will and consciousness, and I will not interfere with your daily existence for the next five days, even at night," Ray made it explicitly clear.

"No, they're being stubborn once more. You know what your lovingly sweet mother said: "I would not let you use Serah's body for even a minute if you were that cruel to us." (She imitated our mother's voice.) I despised her because I was her child as well, but she refused to love me. She wanted me to vanish with no trace of myself. " Ray sounded angry this time.

You little dumb shit could not take all the bullying you had as a child. You used me as a shield to forget all those memories, and you went on living happily as if I did not exist, leaving all the pain to me. (WHAT! I was bullied as a child and have no recollection of it; I was perplexed.) Our parents knew everything, every single stinking thing, but never addressed it. "I could not stand having those bad emotions centred on me, so I set out to make them disappear and give them the worst possible death," said Ray's eyes welled up with tears. "I'll be clear. I didn't kill them; I forced them to kill themselves," she sounded pure wicked, not even a hint of fear on her face.

"I point a little knife at my throat, and the work is done." I made our mother cut our father's throat and nail his hand to the wall. It was really satisfying to see our mother lament, plead, and beg. It was the most amazing day I'd ever experienced. Of course, I've given our father a few face punches, he totally deserves them. "You know, he tried meeting several doctors and slipping different drugs into your meals. That made me weak," she said proudly, as if she had accomplished something fantastic.

"Oh, talking about our beautiful mother, I took matters into my own hands, assisting her in having a more agonising death. BANG! BANG! I smack her head on the wall. I guess twice. Yes, two times. Then she sat down in the chair and we talked for a few minutes. She was referring to you, Serah, without even giving the slightest importance to my presence. She said you were inside and still listening to her. Tch! She did not know you were stupid and frail. The poor woman! Would you like to hear her last words? Here you go, Serah! Take care! She would have been alive here if she hadn't said your name. I stabbed her in the throat as soon as I heard your name from her mouth. I couldn't stand it any longer. The favouritism they'd shown, the backing they'd given to such a weakling like you for years. I've put up with it for a long time, hoping they'd understand and let me out or help me. I was definitely mistaken; they never loved me.

So, they deserve this. Ray concluded her statement without any trace of shame.

"Oh, and don't rush to get the knife; it's the same one Sara used to kill herself." I hid it under the plant our mother planted in the garden the day before her death, after killing her, and brought it back to Sara. See, I told you I'm smart, and yes, and yes, I've got to thank you for not letting the cops find the knife sooner. I located the camera in our house, and it's already being trashed. Now, Dear Serah, you have no choice except to strike a deal with me and live according to what I say. You can't go on, it's clearly a hollow threat. You must murder yourself if you are to end my life. I don't think you're brave enough to accomplish it. So, let us have our happily ever after. Until next time!" Ray finished with a cunning expression.

CHAPTER TEN

ONE LAST TIME

My heart shattered into millions of pieces after hearing all that Ray had said. Ray's triumphant expressions disgusted me the most. I didn't want her to win.

I was puzzled about how to stop Ray's delight, but re-watching her video recording again and again had given me an idea. As the drugs were ineffective, I had no choice but to take matters into my own hands.

She pretended to be intelligent, but she had given me a hint about how to end her life. Yes, I'm going to accomplish exactly what she thought I'd never be able to do.

Even though I was afraid, I decided it was the end, and staring into the mirror, I stated in a darkly serious voice, "You are the only one who can end it, brace yourself up, we'll do it."

Sooner or later, I will be a burden to my aunt and uncle. Furthermore, I am unsure of my ability to protect them from Ray. When Ray takes control, anything may happen. Today is the day I must act before someone else loses their life.

I wanted to say goodbye to my aunt and thank her for everything she and my uncle had done for us since we were little.

When I went out of the room, she was seated in the living room, re-watching her favourite television show while peeling the peas. I sat next to her. I was unsure where to begin.

"How are you now?" she said before I could respond. "Did you get enough rest?" Still watching television.

"Eh! Yes!" I replied.

"That's wonderful to hear," she added, smiling.

"Aunt, I... have to tell you something," I said.

"Yes, dear, continue." She spoke lightly.

"Thank you, thank you, thank you for everything," I said this without hesitation or stopping.

My aunt stopped pealing and looked at me, saying, "Yes, is anything wrong? Did something happen? "Talk to me; I'll help you," hastily and worriedly.

"Oh, no, no, no, I'm well; it's just that you and my uncle have always taken care of us, and I wanted to thank you." I dropped my head down, feeling bad for telling the half-truth.

"Don't be ridiculous; I'm your mother and you're my daughter; don't make me a third person now by introducing formalities in the middle." "Auntie," she remarked in a loving, motherly tone.

Tears welled up in my eyes as I mumbled, "I love you" and held her.

"Oh! "I love you, too," she said as she kissed me on the cheek, stroking my hair and removing a few strands of hair from my face.

I stood up and returned to the room, waving goodbye to my aunt.

She returned the wave.

Back in my room, I cried to myself for deciding to leave behind Aunt and Uncle. It wasn't easy, but I had no choice.

Guilt filled me up for lying to my aunt.

I decided to leave a letter and the video tapes describing all that had happened. I finished the letter and I placed it in the drawer of my reading table.

I took one of my dupattas out of my luggage, drew a chair, stepped on it, tied the dupatta to the fan, and fastened it tightly. I wrapped it around my neck and tightened it at the other end.

It's a tough decision, but there's no other way to punish the monster who murdered my entire family. I can't manage her; she wanted to be free, and I can't let her live her life after what she did to my family. Only the most courageous can choose death; it is not an easy decision. I'd gladly die if I had to go down to bring Ray down.

"I'm sorry, mom and dad," I said as my final but second words.

My ultimate last words were "Let's die together."

****

This is my story.

This is the end of Serah Purushottam.

Note From Author

I shall never forget the process of writing and delivering this book to you. This is my first piece of art and was entirely inspired by a fleeting thought I had one summer night. I hope you enjoyed the narrative.

I wish you and your family health and happiness.

Rajeshwari Andanagiri

9 798887 496337

Printed by Libri Plureos GmbH in Hamburg, Germany